MOON
SNAKE

KIRSTEN ALENE

ERASERHEAD PRESS
PORTLAND, OREGON

ERASERHEAD PRESS
P.O. BOX 10065
PORTLAND, OR 97296

WWW.ERASERHEADPRESS.COM

ISBN: 978-1-62105-242-5

CONTENTS

MOON
SNAKE

"I am a river down in the valley. Oh, I am a vision and I can see clearly." —R. Kelly

For my sister

THE RED BRIDGE IS FINISHED

On the day the red bridge is finished, they catch a blue shark in Seawater Bay. It is the largest blue shark on record and the first to be caught in seven years from the rocky ocean waters of Seawater Bay. When they pull up the blue shark people gasp and sigh. It is what people do when they are pleased and amazed. And the boson on the tall ship that drags the blue shark to shore exclaims: "It's a sign! It's a sign that the red bridge is finished." That is how the people all know that this is the day that the red bridge is finished. That is how the people know that the red bridge is done.

This is all nonsense, of course. Blue sharks have never cared for our bridge building. In fact they know nothing about architecture, as far as anyone knows. But it's no use telling that to a boson. It's no use telling that to the people gathered around. Everyone wants to gasp and sigh in pleasure and amazement. Everyone wants to believe that the red bridge is finished.

MY FATHER, MY FATHER

We have labored on the red bridge for a long time. Pecan Black, my friend, has labored on the red bridge and I, myself, have labored on the red bridge. Sometimes people have to do the things they'd rather not do, for whatever reason. Pecan Black learned this and I learned this and we keep learning.

Seawater Bay is white-capped when they pull the blue shark ashore, beneath the bloody incision of the red bridge on the grayish fleshy coastline. The boson is at the front, his men are at the back. Everyone is pushing and pulling the blue shark, who is dead.

"Did it say anything before you brought it in?" asked Pecan Black.

It is a strange question to ask. Pecan Black is full of strange questions, but a sailor holding a gaff has an answer: "Yes, with its eyes a bit. It said, 'My father, my father.'"

Pecan Black nods solemnly. This makes sense to him. He looks at me, he looks at the sailor, we all three look at each other. We all three look at the blue shark. The blue shark is not saying anything else today. Or ever.

The people gather in the shadow of the red bridge where it is cool. No one knows where the red bridge leads. The last work crews went out four years ago and have not returned. Perhaps now that the red bridge is finished, they never will.

JAMES

When Pecan Black was a child, and I was a child, we had a dog between us named James.

We fed table scraps to James in the evenings. We ran around with James in the day. For a time this carried on. And it turned out James was not so much a dog as a lion cub who one day grew into a lion. We were foolish then and small and a dog is a dog is a dog to anyone as foolish as Pecan Black and myself.

James's taste for human flesh became apparent around the same time as his beard.

James's beard was a wild, straw-colored tangle on his muscle-rich body.

In this week of changes, James ate a porter at a hotel downtown. Luggage and all. James ate a substantial portion of Pecan Black's left arm. Wrist watch and all. James ate a politician and a hot dog seller. Cart and all. James had indigestion, but he seemed so pleased what could we say? We brought James table scraps, but table scraps would no longer do. We brought James fresh, rare steaks from our parents' freezers. But fresh rare steaks would no longer do. James expressed an interest in eating all the rest of Pecan Black.

And it became clear that James would eat us as soon as eat our hot dog vendors. Cart and all.

The people in the town were disgruntled.

They thought, "How could we have had this lion in our midst for so long as a dog that two small children played with?"

They thought, "What will we do without a hot dog vendor, porter, politician and one left arm of a child?"

They thought, "We are now missing three and one-fifths people, all of whom served vital functions in our community."

They thought of who to blame. "We have only ourselves to blame," they thought.

Distraught and guilty, the people confronted James.

The people held no ill will toward James. They thought they understood the situation he was in. They thought they sympathized to some degree, even Pecan Black, now one-armed and wonderful.

"Lion," said the people, "it's time we did what we should have done three years ago when you were just a harmless pet dog named James who ate table scraps in the evenings and ran around in the day."

James looked worried. James looked worried at Pecan Black. James looked worried at me. James looked worried at the space where the hot dog vendor used to sell his hot dogs, just a block or so away.

"I'm sorry," he said, "for what it's worth I can say it will not happen again."

But the people had trouble believing him. Maybe it was his glowing eyes, or his muscle-rich body, or his smooth and massive bulk, maybe it was the way he grinned a little as he picked his teeth with the femur of a politician.

"No," they said, regretfully, "it's time. This is for the best."

The people rushed at James and pulled him by the ears to the then-partially finished red bridge. "Go," they said, "go on across this red bridge and never turn around."

To Pecan Black and me, it seemed like James had a good and honest think about eating a large portion of the people standing around him. But he belched a little from indigestion and maybe he thought better of it. Because then he straightened his beard, he hitched up his tail and he whispered goodbye to me, and to the other nice edible pieces of Pecan Black that he was leaving behind. "Come find me one day when the red bridge is finished," he said. And he walked off down the red bridge.

That is how James became the first person (or lion) to walk out on the red bridge and never return. Many would follow. And none would return.

SOME HARD WORK,
BUT REWARDING

On the day in question, with the red bridge complete and the grey and whiteish waters of Seawater Bay teeming with other sharks than blue sharks, but also blue sharks, Pecan Black and I go about our jobs like we do every day. Our jobs are different but similar enough that if one of us is tired of their job, he or she can do the other job and let his or her job be done by the other one of us. This is how it is done today. I am doing Pecan Black's job. I am counting pear blossoms. It is hard work, but rewarding, as you might expect. I enjoy the sound of numbers under my breath. I enjoy the feel of tacky petals that sometimes brush against my cheeks.

Pecan Black is doing my job. He is separating grains of rice from their papery husks. He counts them as he goes, out of habit. He says it is hard work, but rewarding as you might expect. He enjoys the soft feel of the shells sticking to his fingers, how smooth they make everything, and uniform.

MOON SNAKE

Today, on the day the red bridge is finished and the day when Pecan Black and I go about our jobs, I learn of a place called Moon Snake and Pecan Black learns of a place called Moon Snake, and some other people who happened to be around also learn of it, but I can't speak for what they will do or not do with the information.

In a way it is James who leads us to Moon Snake. In a way it is our imaginations. In other ways, it is just a coincidence. Pecan Black's phantom left arm is often pointing things out to us that we otherwise would never see. Today, it is a hatch in the base of a pear tree with a rope pull for a handle and a little golden plaque which says: Moon Snake.

How it happens is that Pecan Black comes up from the rice field and surprises me in the pear orchard. He is always surprising people. It is one of his great qualities. His one arm snakes around the back of me like a snug, warm seatbelt and his chin rests on my hot ear.

I finish counting the branch I am on, "32, 33, and 34." It is important to be precise with things like pear blossoms. For one day the pear blossoms will be pears. And one day the pears will be pear juice which is the most vital and important substance that we have. More vital and important than any other fruit juice. More vital and important than seawater from Seawater Bay.

We eat sandwiches and leftover squash lasagna. As I am unsnapping the Tupperware lid of the last sandwich, Pecan Black follows the pointing of his phantom left arm with his eyes. I can always tell when his left arm is pointing, even though it is invisible now, having been digested by James so many years ago. In its phantom state it is still a child's arm, with fat round fingers and a scab on the elbow.

I can tell when it is pointing, because Pecan Black looks the way he is looking now.

We rise and follow the direction that it indicates. We follow the arm around the pear orchard to a scraggly old pear tree with barely any blossoms and a gnarled scabby stump where lightning might have once struck it, or someone hacked at it with an axe for whatever reason.

Among the reaching roots and scabs is the door to Moon Snake.

"Should we go in?" says Pecan Black.

Another blossom counter looks over my shoulder. "Best not," he says.

"I'd say no," says someone else, "it looks cramped."

I whisper to Pecan Black that maybe it opens up on the other side, anything could be through the door to Moon Snake. I say, "Let's come back later."

And that is how Pecan Black and I find Moon Snake.

AFTER THE LAST SANDWICH

When our jobs are done and our last sandwich is eaten, Pecan Black and I stretch out on a hill above the red bridge. We watch the people down below, scurrying around, not quite brave enough yet, but almost ready to go out on the sturdy wooden planks that stretch off as far as the eye can see. We watch the people thinking, "Will we ever go out on the red bridge?" Thinking, "Will we ever cross the red bridge?" Thinking, "If the red bridge is done, how long will it be before the last workers come back, or will they ever come back across the red bridge?"

Pecan Black, my friend, came back across, as did I, myself. But that was long ago, when bearded people were beardless and no one knew of Moon Snake and no one hated James, and James was never born.

The hill above the red bridge has no rice or pear blossoms, just sun rays and many shadows. Some explained, some unexplained.

SHAMAN

By the time the shaman calls, birds have begun to wake us and our sleepiness is retreating like a wary animal who senses a predator. The shaman is not the predator of our sleep. The predator of our sleep is our own hot bodies baking in the star light.

"Pecan Black, Pecan Black," calls the shaman through the window. Shamans almost never call through doors, or knock on doors, or stand near them at all. It is a thing we learn early on, that the port of entry for a shaman is the window. Though we only have the one shaman to inform us of their habits.

"Pecan Black, Pecan Black," the shaman knocks with every syllable of the name I know better than my own. He is knocking on the window pane, which is made of sugar glass and rattles ominously with every knock.

Pecan Black and I live on either side of a large avocado tree. Where the one branch forms a platform, there together we built Pecan Black's house and where another forms a V shape, there together we built mine. My house is cantilevered from the outer limb and sways in heavy wind. I am suspended because I am so much lighter than Pecan Black, who is not suspended. Our houses meet in one long room. The window we share is being beat in by a shaman.

I look out the door of my cantilevered house and

say, "Shaman, it is barely sunrise."

The shaman wants to speak to Pecan Black.

"Alright," I say, and I cross back over to the warm space I left beside the scooped-in body of Pecan Black. "Alright," I say. I let the shaman in through the window to discuss his business with Pecan Black.

The shaman is close to his dreams. In the shaman's dreams he is a sailor, sailing a wooden boat across Seawater Bay, in a perpetual sunset that pinkens his dark cheeks and lightens his dark eyes. The boat is made of wood, and its sails are woven from pear blossoms and a big steam engine roars and moans below decks, fueled by herbal remedies and magic potions.

Pecan Black is helping the shaman build the dream boat. It is a community service and someone must do it. That someone is Pecan Black.

I put on coffee. I pull on a sweater. The sky is dark. The shaman sits down on the bed beside the rumpled, half-woken form of Pecan Black and tells him what progress has been made in brewing the magic potions that will propel the dream vessel when it is completed. Pecan Black is unimpressed that I have opened our window to a shaman in the night.

MOON SNAKE

When we go through the door to Moon Snake, a terrible sight awaits us.

At first a long and narrow passage that leads down and out the side of a nonexistent hill. Pecan Black must crawl along, and I must bend in a half moon. The way is clear, the dirt is beaten down by many feet.

The other side of the bridge, the end of the red bridge, is a cold metal line, cutting through this foreign shore.

The water is not the white-capped endlessness of Seawater Bay. The hillsides are bare and rocky. No one is there. No one is alive.

Brownish moss covers everything, even our toes as we stand still upon the heath. When we step up and over the rocks, moss tendrils stretch and snap.

We see the red bridge strewn with corpses of the workers, the sun-bleached bones of a lion, and black birds still feeding on the arms of men.

We reach the other side of the red bridge. Pecan Black and I. It is called Moon Snake and it is terrible.

BREAD AND JAM

While Pecan Black beats on the wooden sides of the dream boat, the shaman serves me bread and jam. Bread and jam, bread and jam. I smack my lips in time to the sounds of Pecan Black's hammer.

A SHORTAGE OF PEAR BLOSSOMS

I read a report published in the newspaper. The report is concerned with pear blossoms. There is a shortage of pear blossoms, based on recent figures collected by the Pear Blossom Bureau (who is Pecan Black's employer), and that means, the report states, a shortage of pears is coming. This means, the report further conjectures, a shortage of pear juice will soon be upon us.

A SISTER WEAVES ILLICIT
PEAR BLOSSOMS

Across town, I visit my sister. Her house is underground, much like Moon Snake, and I crouch into a dreaded half moon to scurry through the peaty tunnel and down into her sitting room.

"Tell me everything you know about the red bridge," she says from behind a wall of pear blossoms, "and tell me quick."

AN INVISIBLE ARM

Pecan Black's muscular back is arched. He is lifting a large timber into place with one invisible arm and one visible arm. We both know the invisible arm is powerless, but when he is working on the shaman's dream boat, it comes to life. It steadies logs and hammers nails, and sometimes holds a glass of pear juice for Pecan Black's lips to drink from.

I want to ask him, "Why is my sister weaving a sail of pear blossoms?" I want to ask him, "Why is there a shortage of pear blossoms that could lead to a shortage of pears that could lead to a shortage of pear juice that could threaten the health and comfort of all the people we know, even us?"

Do I think my beloved friend Pecan Black is a suspect in this pear blossom crime? No. But if anyone could give my sister a host of fresh pear blossoms to weave carefully into a sail, it would be me or Pecan Black. Am I a suspect in this pear blossom crime? Perhaps.

REAL ESTATE VALUE
OF THE AVOCADO HOMES

When people come to visit us that aren't the shaman, they enter through our doors. "My my!" They often say, "My my look at what you've done here. How charming."

'How charming' is a way for some people to say, 'Oh no, I am uncomfortable and confused,' where 'charming' can mean 'odd' or 'strange,' and the people are flushed and sweaty. Some people.

Not all people, and certainly not the shaman. The shaman says only what he means, and he only says anything to Pecan Black.

The shaman looks very nice in our avocado homes. He fits in a corner where we haven't anything else, he fits in the chairs and looks fine in the kitchen.

When the people look around inside these avocado tree homes, they don't approve. They think our kitchens are small and cramped. They think our bedrooms are large and indulgent. They think our tin roofs are homely and our cardboard siding is cheap. They don't understand that it never rains except from above, and the cardboard is breezy in the summer heat. Where are the closets, they ask. Where is the off-street parking. What is the property value going to be like in ten years. How do you manage this queer, multi-level living space. Is all of your furniture 'custom.' Where is the billiards table meant to go. The television. The duck pond.

Our avocado homes are not a sound real estate investment.

A SISTER WEAVES ALONE

In my next life, I will either be a moth or a donkey cart driver. My mother always said, "Nothing as sad as a moth that thinks it's found the moon in a candle flame." And that is who I am, or who I am meant to have been. I whisper under my breath, "Moon in a candle flame, moon in a candle flame." And it's true. It's sad but also beautiful.

So I'm not scared.

If I am not a moth, surely I will be a donkey cart driver with two fit brown steeds and gleaming leather harnesses and all.

I'm sure of these things as I am sure of nothing else. It means I am safe to weave this pear blossom sail for what I know to be a good cause. At worst, I will be a moth or a donkey cart driver.

A THREATENING MISSIVE

On Sundays the elephant milk delivery is dropped at the base of our avocado tree. Today, the elephant milk delivery man leaves a threatening missive.

"Dear sir or madam, we know where the pear blossoms are. We know who you are. We know what you are doing. We know how to stop you. We know everything."

The letter is signed, "Sincerely, anonymous."

The elephant milk delivery man is seen creeping about the base of the avocado tree long after his delivery has been made.

Pecan Black crawls down the ladder in his underwear. We hear a snigger from the bushes.

Pecan Black is an embarrassed maroon when he re-enters the avocado homes we share, clutching the cartons of elephant milk and scowling around at all our furniture.

SHAMAN

Could it be me, myself, who is unknowingly responsible for this heinous theft of pear blossoms? Should I try to bring myself to suspect the one-armed, wondrous Pecan Black?

Should I suspect you, shaman?

The shaman is silent, as usual. He nods appreciatively. He could be meditating. Or listening. Or dead. The nod could be a breeze rustling past.

I watch for a pulse in his neck somewhere, expect to see a small vein throbbing, but see nothing to indicate he is alive.

Or listening.

He seems to nod again.

Or is this theft even really a theft? Perhaps those pear blossoms were accidental acquisitions. Fallen blossoms that accumulated in a capable hand day after day, blossoms that never would have bloomed to pears. That never would have been pear juice. That never would have been counted.

In my hand is the scrunched-up note. The accusation that I plucked from the elephant milk as Pecan Black rummaged angrily for pants.

Once those bare thighs of Pecan Black signified nothing to me. Now they are like the candle flame a moth chases when it mistakes the fire for the moon.

ANOTHER PECAN BLACK

I spend time wondering if there is another Pecan Black,
when all signs point toward a heist of pear blossoms.
Another Pecan Black, two-armed and terrible.

A SISTER POURS TEA

"It was a bridge once only partially completed. Now it appears to be done," I begin. "Further than that I know only that the red bridge is terrible. That the red bridge is fearful. That I am scared of the red bridge now."

Even though I know I have not been followed into the rabbit hole of my sister's home, I look around and around again. She is just alone, weaving such careful and loving knots of pear blossoms for what we all know must be the greater good. The question I fear to ask is the question I ask as my sister pours our tea, one finger in the cup to keep from overfilling. "Where did you get all of these pear blossoms?"

She smiles nervously. I think she is dematerializing in the light from the one little window in the ceiling. Dust and pear pollen billow out from her apron when she straightens it.

"Oh those." She wipes her wrist across her forehead, which is her way. "They come down the chimney to me. Like snow. They pile up on the flue."

I mean to say, 'Who brings them?' But my words are smokey in my throat.

"I think," she says, "I think the wind blows them in. I'm sure the wind is doing it."

Dust and pear pollen, shady light, and the steam from the tea pot conspire to make my sister invisible.

Do I even have a sister? However I found myself here, maybe I am inventing sisters. Then she reappears. Phew.

"Who brings them here? Who brings you the pear blossoms?"

"I don't know."

AN ATTEMPT TO TAMPER
WITH EVIDENCE / A SLUG FLOOR

The secretary is a stern old woman. The secretary is a largemouth bass.

Her eyes are glassy and knowing. Her mouth opens slowly and with purpose, like she is meditating. Her front fins curl and uncurl according to a deep internal rhythm.

We sit in silence for a while. People bustle outside and things clank and clunk on the other side of the frosted glass door that stands between the smallmouth bass and the offices of the newspaper. Behind that door they are printing the paper. Behind that door they are writing and editing and chopping and adding and framing and inking and stamping and cutting and folding and packaging and billing and collecting and distributing and calling and writing and writing and writing.

Outside, we are waiting.

"We have a spot for eleven words. Ninety characters. No more. No less."

I blink.

"And a by-line. Two words. Your name, your name."

I am not here to write eleven words for the paper.

When I am young I have a certainty that I will one day be a writer. I look at pens and pencils with judgmental hawk eyes. I consider typewriters, I consider their carriage returns and their weight. I compare paper grades and thicknesses of ink.

My serious nature and the serious nature of Pecan Black indicate a serious future where I am a writer and he is a bookmaker and we create and distribute these wares we make together from a serious office on one limb of the avocado tree. We spend many hours discussing this inevitability, carefully molding what we perceive to be our individual talents to compliment the talents we perceive in each other.

We also collect big piles of brown slugs after it rains, and spread them like seeds on the moss carpet of our bedrooms. We want a slug floor. Oh what joy a slug floor would bring.

But I am not here to think about the slug floor (or how nice it would have been). I am not here to think about how, before James, I would have been the writer that this newspaper needed and not a simple rice counter.

I am here to clear the name of Pecan Black. I am here to find the report, to change the numbers, to somehow make all of this untrue.

The bass secretary polishes a monocle and opens a filing cabinet.

"Here we are."

She drops a folder on the desk between us. The folder emits a cloud of pear pollen and dust as it slaps the desk.

I reach through the dust with both hands.

"It's a copy."

I did not want a copy. I did not think about copies. Copies are the opposite of the situation I envisioned happening when I entered this office, sat down before the bass secretary, and made my demands.

Copies.

I flip through the pages and I see a familiar name and I experience a familiar memory, which is the memory of a person lifting timbers onto the dream boat with one visible and one invisible arm.

THE BACKWARDS TIME

Will we be able to run our electric trolleys and our little personal coffee makers with a shortage of pear juice? Will we be able to run our fountains in the public squares, the printing presses in our newspaper office, or our fossil research center with a pear juice shortage?

Where will the cutbacks begin, and who will decide? People ask each other these questions.

I am overcome with excitement.

Once my sister and I rode backwards together in a station wagon. The road stretched away, racing back from us at unquantifiable speeds. The glass of the hatch was mildewed and foggy, but other drivers saw us. They waved to us. Their passengers were dogs sometimes, and other children. I struggle to remember this backwards time. I think of it often. How the narrow seat between us held pear blossoms. How the fuel of the car was pear blossoms and the formula in our bottles was pear blossoms and the radio signals we received were channeled with pear blossoms and the tires that carried us were forged from pear blossoms. How our infant hands clasped pear blossoms, clasped them all together.

THE IMMEASURABLE GRIEF
OF PECAN BLACK

When James's narrow haunches passed into the mist on the red bridge and his swinging velvet tail brushed into the darkness, Pecan Black was filled with sadness. Others tried to comfort him. They said: "Now at least you get to keep your remaining limbs." But what they did not understand is that Pecan Black would have gladly forfeit all those limbs and any others to keep our James for us, to keep him with us, prowling around the avocado homes and sleeping peaceful by our beds.

SLUG CONGRESS

The slug floor never sprouted like we thought, the seeds we planted did not take hold. But years later a congress was held on our bare mossy floor, a congress by other slugs to honor their ancestors and remember those slugs who had gone before them, to preserve their heritage.

We were so impressed by the gravity, and so pleased with their presence that we offered them the space on a biannual basis, free of charge. Now they come regularly, in growing numbers, to the floors of our avocado homes and they crawl on our toes and all around our furniture, making the slight but pleasant sounds all slugs make, and leaving their glistening star trails behind them.

When I get home from the newspaper office, Pecan Black is serving hot elephant milk by the thimble and tiptoeing around their sausagey bodies. We clamber into a hammock strung from the ceiling to try to be out of their way. And we hold ourselves against ourselves until we are just one Pecan Black.

MOON SNAKE

The sidewalks in Moon Snake are smooth and even. They are all one colorless color, and no grass grows between the stones. Some sidewalks lead over grassy hills, some lead under the red bridge and out into the water that is not Seawater Bay. Some sidewalks meet with other sidewalks in perpendicular crosses, but some sidewalks continue alone, flat lengths of ribbon all unwound from the same roll.

The thing about sidewalks in Moon Snake is that they are traveled evenly. Worn grooves appear down the exact center of each sidewalk like a walker has walked them all with an even, deliberate stride, over and over, for a century.

The thing about sidewalks here is that there are no sidewalks. People walk around, but they walk over hills or in the grass, they leap over small streams without bridges, sometimes they stop to clamber up a tree or meet a neighbor or scratch the head of a donkey or run around a good-looking clearing in the forest. The thing about sidewalks here is that no one needs them and no one misses them.

We think about the curious person, or people, of Moon Snake. How they are never diverted but walk always in one straight and curving line, never listing to one side or the other, or stopping to touch the grass or climb into a tree or watch a sunset or splash in a puddle or bathe in the strange and greenish water of the not-Seawater Bay.

We think if there are two inhabitants here, they never meet, or more than two, they never meet, and how lonely the sidewalks of Moon Snake feel to us. How they are so lonely.

THE STORY OF BRUTAL FRUIT
AND KNOWING ABOUT LIES

If someone lied, we would forgive them, the theft of
pear blossoms is a subject far more worrisome than a
lie. A lie is just words and feelings, but a pear blossom
is a real living thing.

I will tell you about a person who I have known, a
person who I have known to lie.

The person I call Brutal Fruit by virtue of the fact
this is his name. Brutal Fruit was once long-bearded
and wove tiny twigs and rocks he found into bangles in
the hair of his long beard but never sold them so that
every bangle was still in the hair of his long beard like an
ornament and so that they clanked and banged together
with a friendly, frantic sound when Brutal Fruit was near.

Brutal Fruit was a thief. The items he thieved were
various and included, but were not limited to: cutlery,
candlesticks, mirrors, flags and pendants, pen sets, locks
of hair, bananas, toenail clippings, suspenders, various
fruit other than bananas, an idol, a watch, a hedgerow,
pennies or pelts.

When Brutal Fruit clanged by, chances were an item
you once had would be gone.

When asked, he was heard to blame a porcupine which
no one ever saw, but which he claimed was attracted to
gold and silver. He often blamed a child which no one

ever knew, whom he claimed had sinister connections and wore a paisley hat. From time to time, Brutal Fruit would bend right over in shame and horror and blame a minister he called Minister Moon Snake—a sickly man with greenish flesh who only Brutal Fruit could see.

He told us, "Moon Snake, Moon Snake the minister of the underworld, the protector of the dead, the guard and keeper of the blackberry gates."

That Moon Snake thieved and blamed the thefts on Brutal Fruit, sometimes I think now, must be true.

Brutal Fruit would throw his hairy body down before us, his accusers, and fling the bangles from his beard around and gaze into our eyes and weep with us, too, for whatever had been lost.

I do not have to tell you of the fate of Brutal Fruit, which even after his treachery and thievery and lies, still makes us scared and pitying where we were executors before.

I do not have to tell you of the terrible fate of Brutal Fruit, of the cutting of his beard and the trimming of his bangles and the weeping of his eyes and the sad explosions of his heart and the solemn padding of his feet as we led him, pink faced and stumbling, to the red bridge and said, "Go."

I do not have to tell you that we all know what a lie is now, and I do not have to tell you that the punishment of liars is sometimes not a punishment, and sometimes of course a lie is not a lie, or even a whole lie if it is a lie.

In the tangles of his beard trimmings people found their mirrors and their cutlery, and their long lost dinner plates and their bananas brown with age, but no one found the things they missed the most, and no one ever does, and they left their once-possessions in the shaven tangles and watched the misty shadow of Brutal Fruit go.

ANOTHER PECAN BLACK

Pecan Black is working on the dream boat again and I am helping with the planking.

From here I can watch Pecan Black move and use his invisible arm like it is reattached. He is taking measurements and smoking a cigar. The cigar hovers at his side, then rises deftly to his lips and he inhales. These are the symptoms of having an actual arm. I should know.

Pecan Black will mention nothing.

His silence is a message that says: "Maybe pear blossoms are missing, and maybe people are angry, but two arms are better than one."

Then in the night I feel a hand on my cheek and that hand is Pecan Black's, but it is not the hand I know. He is awake and staring at me in the night. He gestures with his visible hand, he gestures to the weight I feel and he finally says: "Can you feel that?"

I clasp the invisible hand, which is a child's hand, and feel my stomach churn.

MOON SNAKE

In Moon Snake, alone, I finally understand the shadows I have seen when Pecan Black and I lay out upon the hill where no pears grow and no rice needs to be counted. Now when I lay there, there is no Pecan Black beside me, one-armed or otherwise. He is engaged deep in the engine of the dream boat and I am counting both our jobs. Rice in the evening and pear blossoms through the day. And they are right. There is a shortage. A grave and notable shortage of pear blossoms.

As I sit before the red bridge in Moon Snake, my chest will rise and fall heavily. It is the only movement in any chest, for the only other occupants of Moon Snake are sad, stretching their limbs toward me on the shore, but never reaching or touching. Not even touching each other.

I sit alone in Moon Snake now and I look at them and they look at me and their bodies are still and missing pieces and I am fidgeting but whole.

THE SHAMAN TELLS A JOKE

An antelope in a bar sees a man she doesn't know and he buys her a drink like a gentleman. He introduces himself and tells her he is a cheetah. They finish their drinks and have a game of pool. When she isn't looking, he walks around the table and pockets all his stripes. The antelope turns around and sees the table looks different. The man shrugs, then leaps across the table and devours the antelope in front of all the other patrons.

SHAMAN

The shaman hangs wind chimes from the avocado tree and stands back to admire his work. They clang and clang their hollow tubes together in a deafening racket. He sleeps easier at night knowing he has caused this noise to happen.

The wind is grateful that the shaman has given it a voice and it spares the avocado homes when it rips down other people's houses, tearing up their doors and flying up their sashes and fluffing down their chimneys with clouds of ash and refuse.

The wind brings a pear blossom right to my open palm as I crouch in the doorway of my avocado house, cantilevered off the edge of the tree. My house and I sway gently with the musical gusts and I wonder at the sleeping shaman in the grass below, his greenish flesh and spindly form. And I wonder if, in any light, the shaman and Moon Snake are one.

ANOTHER PECAN BLACK

Pecan Black is growing like a dandelion, two-armed and terrible.

THE IMMEASURABLE GRIEF
OF PECAN BLACK

The grief of Pecan Black could, at one time, not have been measured. His pity was so extreme, his heart an empty saucer with a hundred kittens licking round in hunger. The whole of Pecan Black was tragedy and only I could reach him in the swamp of his despair. And when I reached him I was helpless. An impossible pressure weighed on us and we could not lift it with just three arms.

If the shaman had been here then, our fourth arm would have pried us loose but instead we stayed and stayed together. We thought of James and how we used to feed him table scraps and run around in daytime.

Our families looked at us and wept and our brothers and our sisters did not know us and feeling our heaviness was all we did until they were gone and only we remained, weeping at each other and recognizing nothing.

Then we grew.

We grew taller, a little wider, and then taller still. The ceiling of our sadness rose as our spines lengthened.

We left the doors of the avocado houses open and the windows cracked at night to let in starlight, breezes and mosquitos, which bit our swampy flesh and brought us back into the living world.

When I think of where we might have been, I think of Moon Snake, though we didn't know it then, but no one knew it then. But no one for years could find us until we grew out of that darkness that Pecan Black forged from all his sadness.

By the time we truly emerged, fresh-faced and watermelon-scented, the missing arm of Pecan Black was nothing and he missed it not at all and could do all the things that needed doing with just the one.

When the doors opened up on the avocado house, it was too late for us to be children and too late for me to be a writer. It was too late for people to want to give us time to rest or acclimate or grow into our new bodies. It was too late for all that.

We got jobs and trimmed back branches and drank pear juice every night.

I wonder for the first time how it would have been without James, how it would have been if Pecan Black had not been found.

I wonder how it would have been without the shaman.

MOON SNAKE

But I never wonder. And cannot wonder. Or even think of how it would have been without Moon Snake.

MY SISTER IS MURDERED EVERYWHERE BUT MOON SNAKE

The only living thing I ever saw in Moon Snake was a moth the size of my palm. She was nestled in the collarbone of a corpse that could have been Brutal Fruit or so many others. She landed on my cheek and walked about there with her corpse feet. She looked just like my sister and I held her gently in the cages of my fingers, watching her flap and fly and twitch all around.

Then again, do I have a sister at all? Or only a person I know who weaves pear blossoms into a sail and pours tea by using her finger as a measure on the inside of the cup.

My sister is blind, already a moth who feels only flame heat and never the cool heat of the moon, even in Moon Snake.

SOME QUESTIONS

Is Pecan Black my friend? Or do I have a friend at all? Or just the people who I know who go around me when we meet each other. Just the people that I know who sleep in houses within sight of the red bridge and always under its spell.

Is my cantilevered home the only home with windows not full of the red bridge over Seawater Bay?

Is Pecan Black at home or in the dream boat with the shaman? Is my sister dead or weaving pear blossoms underground in a tunnel much like Moon Snake (which is another way of saying dead)?

CAPE TOWN,
MAYOR / A PORCUPINE

What some don't know is that we have a mayor and his name is Cape Town. His skin is soft and his eyes are kind but in some lights he is unmistakably the porcupine whom Brutal Fruit once blamed. He has a love of silver things. He has a love of gold things. His quills are visible in moonlight and are as black and white and rich as marbled chocolate.

Cape Town, mayor, speaks to the people on a Tuesday when Pecan Black is in the dream boat, not at home. I go to see Cape Town, mayor, speak because I grow sick whenever I see Pecan Black's new and real invisible arm at work, whether building the dream boat or tying my shoes for me.

Cape Town, mayor, is wise and others are beginning to know of/talk about/look at/find the door to Moon Snake, but they never open it. The mayor will address the mystery of Moon Snake, though not he nor anyone has gone over except for me, Pecan Black, my dead sister, and the shaman.

THE THOUGHTS OF PECAN BLACK

The boat I am building is big enough to carry us all away, to a distant shore that isn't Moon Snake. What I have always wanted is somewhere waiting. What I have always wanted is to be whole. I have a friend who loves me, but now I never see the friend. The friend is somewhere, waiting. I have a wish that the friend will forgive me all the things I've done to build this boat and please the shaman. I have a wish the friend will still love me. I have a friend who loved me. I have a sister of that friend who would do anything I ask. I think the sister of that friend is dead.

MOON SNAKE

One day in Moon Snake I walk across the sidewalks diagonally, watching Pecan Black who does not know that I am here. When we come through separate, I am as invisible as his missing arm.

I watch him step over the threshold of the red bridge that so lured the corpses beyond it and so terrified me before it.

I watch him march toward the corpse bones of a lion. I watch him kick the bones aside and clutch a tibia, some carpels, and a few fragments of what I gather are his arm. He takes them all to him like a new father and he cradles them and gazes at them, and leaves.

CAPE TOWN, MAYOR

"One thing is clear," says Cape Town, mayor, "if we avoid anything, we should avoid this Moon Snake.

"When a thing disappears, we know what to do. When a thing changes suddenly, or transforms before our eyes, we know what to do. But when a thing appears where no thing was before, like that," he snaps his fingers, "then we must respect the nature of that thing, like a shaman, and let it be. We must meet its demands, only, and never make demands of it. Ever.

"Thus I urge you, people, keep well clear of Moon Snake. Forget there is a Moon Snake, sleep peacefully with your windows latched against it."

I respect this opinion of Moon Snake and I wish we'd never found it first, or found it later, or never found it at all.

A guard is placed on Moon Snake and we are trapped on our side. I am glad for us. But the shaman is enraged.

A LONG TIME AGO OR
AT LEAST SEVERAL MONTHS

The shaman is first sighted lying at the very threshold of the red bridge. His sandy feet and greenish toes rest just inches from the first plank. The shadow of his body is long and reaches out across the sand, lapping at the ship-bearing waves of Seawater Bay like it belongs.

Cape Town, mayor, is at first alone, staring blankly at the glittering newborn wetness of the shaman. The shaman is covered in a sand-like outer skin. The shaman is not shivering or cold.

The mayor is distressed and unamused. Other people gather around. Other people take notes and make sketches of the scene for posterity.

Did this shaman come from the other side of the red bridge?

It seems impossible.

The red bridge is not complete.

It seems impossible, but true.

Pecan Black, my friend, bursts through the gathering people. "Did you see a lion? Did you pass a lion on your way?" He screeches, "Did you pass a healthy lion?"

The shaman hasn't seen a lion, but a pet dog of some sort. Someone's pet dog has been on the red bridge, and is maybe still walking, along the planks somewhere.

Pecan Black is on his knees, his one arm bent over his

face and his shoulders shaking. My sister turns toward me, and I turn toward my sister. Other people sigh and tut in confusion.

Cape Town, mayor, releases a low grumble.

The body of the shaman rises and every piece that touched the ground is green. Quickly the pallor fades and the red eyes soften and the fingers unclench until the shaman stands before us, and Pecan Black kneels, and they clasp hands.

INVISIBLE ARM

Pecan Black is up in the night and I feel the floorboards of my home bend beneath his weight. I creep out of my room to watch him silvered by moonlight. He is exercising the invisible arm. He is flexing and unflexing. Lifting and jabbing.

The pieces of bones he gathered at Moon Snake are rattling on the floor, shaking as if they are boiling and clanking together in a pot.

This is how I know I must see my sister. I must see if I still have a sister.

A TERRIBLE THING HAPPENS

I am the one that fears for the life of Pecan Black. But that life is no real life now.

I dream that the body of Pecan Black comes back to me, entwined in my body, but it is just a dream. I wake alone with the smell of bread and pear blossom jam. The window is open and the shaman is making breakfast. He serves me bread and jam. Bread and jam.

The bones of Pecan Black are gone. The bones of my sister are self-burying. As is the pear blossom sail.

The shaman doesn't tell me anything, but I can tell the dream boat is finished. The steam engine roars. I hear it through the open window. I can hear it through the closed door. I can hear it roaring down through the tin roof and the leaves of the avocado tree.

Beneath the avocado tree, people gather around.

Hands sticky with jam, I limp down the ladder to join them and the shaman watches as we crawl toward the dream vessel like slugs.

When we arrive, Pecan Black is searching faces.

He is searching in faces for me. His eyes are magnets for me. His eyes are radar for me.

I remember that I have a friend called Pecan Black. I remember all his deeds and all his faults and all his smells that I have smelled.

There is no sign of the pear blossom sail. The riggings

are empty, the rope ties are free of ropes. But the dream vessel is complete.

People are looking it over.

Cape Town, the mayor, says a blessing in our other, silent language.

People are pleased.

I seem pleased as well, but it is hard to seem anything when pinned by the sewing pin eyes of Pecan Black.

He lifts me with the real arm and enfolds me on the bow.

My memory becomes the only thing that is happening and the people gasp and sigh.

Then the people scream.

One of them, a small one, has climbed the sail-less rigging of the dream boat. The person is a child and the child is falling. Is about to fall. Has already fallen.

A thing then happens that should never have happened and I unclasp myself from Pecan Black's running body.

That body dives over the side of the boat and I watch the invisible arm grab the falling child and hang on.

This is a tragedy worse than a fallen child smooshed out on the grass beneath a dream boat.

I will the child to have already fallen the two feet to the ground but it is suspended. Pecan Black's stump shoulder extending toward it.

No one gasps or sighs.

No one screams.

A gasp or a sigh or a scream would not make sense.

All the people look around. All the people look at me.

They look at Pecan Black. A single pear blossom slips from his breast pocket, and slowly it drips down onto the railing of the boat.

Before he can say, "Let me explain," or "Peanut butter sandwich," or any other helpful sentence, the people are upon him.

Then they all start to weep.

But I will never weep again. Nor will Pecan Black.

Here is what happens when the people see the invisible arm doing its work:

1. They swarm the dream boat.

2. They take Pecan Black.

3. They leave the child behind.

4. They race to the house of the elephant milk delivery man.

(Elephants stand around outside, their backs all sandy and brown with elephant sunscreen.)

5. They all ride elephants to the red bridge.

(Pecan Black is clasped tightly in a trunk.)

6. They stand below and all around the red bridge.

7. The shaman stabs the man who is guarding Moon Snake and wrestles open the locked door.

(This happens far away, and no one sees it happening.)

8. Everyone knows who took the pear blossoms and why there is a pear blossom shortage.

9. Everyone knows how the arm came back.

10. Everyone knows who will drive the dream boat.

11. Everyone knows it is not the shaman. (It is the shaman, but not the shaman.)

12. Everyone knows that Pecan Black is dead.

13. They send the fake Pecan Black, two-armed and terrible, out onto the red bridge. (They say, "Go.")

MY FRIEND, PECAN BLACK

People are cleverer than we think. I want to bury myself in the waves of Seawater Bay. Even though I know that I have never had my friend back, that there is no Pecan Black, I feel a sadness take me over that is more complete than the red bridge was the day they pulled a blue shark from the water.

Tall ships circle out in Seawater Bay. Bosons call to their crews and captains peer at each other through telescopes barely strong enough to pick up the shaman shadow of the Pecan Black who trudges angrily out to Moon Snake.

THE GRAVE OF MY SISTER

The rabbit hole tunnel is collapsed and the sides of the wall are caved in by unmistakable elephant footprints. The moon is bright and full on a few things I recognize: a bottle of milk, a teapot, a silver spoon, broken fragments of a beautiful wooden loom, a lifeless bit of flesh that once was an arm and hand, protruding from the dirt like it is making an escape.

After retching into the bushes, I unfurl the fingers of the hand and clasped inside them is a note: "Dear sir or madam, consider yourself warned." It is signed, "Sincerely, anonymous."

Trampled under the rubble and dirt is a soft whiteness that I recognize.

The pear blossom sail.

I bury it.

SHAMAN / PECAN BLACK / MOON SNAKE

Moon Snake is breached and the shaman is gone.

THE RED BRIDGE IS FINISHED

The avocado tree is in bloom and avocado blossoms feather down to me as I patch and mend the sail. It is part pear blossom now, part bone, part avocado blossom, and part magic.

Without a shaman there will be no magic potions to fuel the steam engine, but I will learn to catch the wind on Seawater Bay. I will learn to turn the sails by myself and roll the boat around to sail with the waves.

I will learn to sail to that other shore. Not our shore. Not the blood-soaked shore of Moon Snake. That other shore where Pecan Black is headed on the red bridge. Where Pecan Black, my friend, is walking even now, one-armed and wonderful, with the pet dog we shared together when we were small.

I SET THE AVOCADO
HOMES ON FIRE

A single large brown moth tears up through the open door from Moon Snake. It is my sister at last.

I set the avocado homes on fire.

The tree is crumbling and it is a testament to the mathematical skills of a young Pecan Black that my cantilevered home is the last to fall, when the weight of the other home finally rises up in billowing smoke and ash to join the smoke and ash of burning leaves and roasting fruits.

Because of the pear blossom shortage, the fire engines have no fuel. No one will come to rescue this avocado tree filled with homes.

Some people watch cautiously. They stand with slugs around and in front of them. All around. And everyone watches.

Except me.

And the moth.

And Pecan Black, who is still walking, probably, nearing the other side of the red bridge. In Moon Snake, or some other place, some other terrible shore.

SHAMAN / MOON SNAKE

One thing can be said for sure: the walker of Moon Snake is walking again. And he will walk forever.

PECAN BLACK

While the avocado tree burns, I race to the shores of Seawater Bay.

The sharks there are circling around waiting for someone to say: "Hey, could you lend a hand?"

"Hey," I call to them, "could you lend a hand?"

Together we push and pull the dream vessel out into the water.

A moth circles the crow's nest.

I clamber up onto the rigging and the pear blossom sail unfurls, glowing hotly in the moonlight.

"Ooooo," say the sharks.

"Ahhhhh," say the sharks.

The winds of Seawater Bay are rising.

The other tall ships haul anchor. They spread out across the bay to give the dream vessel room as she lumbers forward on her amateur hull, listing one way, then the other.

Pecan Black.

Pecan Black.

I want to speak to Pecan Black.

CATHEDRAL
BONE

"There's only one place this road ever ends up and I don't want to die alone." —John Darnielle

For my daughter

MASTIFFS

September I move into the house of mastiffs. I begin volunteering at the cathedral. I can tell you much about the house of mastiffs: a broiling brindle carpet, the slobberous, drooling walls. When I arrive home in the evenings, all the mastiffs say, "Jah," instead of "yes" and they remind me of home.

They remind me of television.

Their septic flat coats.

Their eyes are like crocodile eyes, perched sleepy above their baby-killer jaws.

"How was your day," it is my custom to ask them.

"Jah mistress, Jah ma'am."

When I move among them I can feel their warmth and they can feel mine.

During the day, when I am gone, the blackbirds feed them in the yard. The blackbirds feed them by dropping pecans from the pecan trees that encircle the house.

One pecan here. One pecan there. One hungry mastiff. Two hungry mastiffs. With sleepy, crocodile eyes.

I sleep each night in a hammock of mastiffs.

Mastiffs standing still. Mastiffs swaying gently. Mastiffs munching pecans. Mastiffs holding low murmured conversations.

In the morning mastiffs wake me and I take them for a walk. Everyone flees before us as the mastiffs flood the parks and streets.

Blackbirds above, mastiff droppings beneath, and me in the middle.

"Where do all those mastiffs come from?" people shout to me as I try to wrangle all the mismatched extendable leads. Their shoulders are elbow height and dipping up and down like mastiff shoulders do until I look like I am in the middle of a mastiff ocean, clinging to a mastiff boat, in the eye of a mastiff storm.

"I'm not sure!" I shout back. I am not sure where they come from. That is the truth.

"Jah!" The mastiffs laugh and bark, "Jah, mistress!"

I toss them some pecans from the blackbird at my side.

BAPTISMAL MASTIFF

I am volunteering at the cathedral by accident.

There is a lot of paperwork involved. The priest gives me crayons and a crayon sharpener. "Finish these here," he says.

I attempt to explain that there's been a mistake. I just needed directions to the cinema. The priest just needed a volunteer. We happened to each other at the wrong time.

One mastiff has managed to escape and follow me here. He is drooling in the baptismal font.

"Stop that!" I hiss.

"Jah!" he says which, contradictorily, means no.

It is useless to be strict with mastiffs. They act only for their own pleasure.

The priest is spying on us from the balcony. He pretends to tune the pipe organ.

I fill out the paperwork in crayon. I am not concerned about the legibility. This is not a real job. I am only volunteering.

"Jah," someone whispers next to me. I jump. It is only the mastiff.

He is reading over my shoulder.

"I would read the fine print," he says.

But I am not concerned with the fine print. This is not a real job. I am only volunteering.

And I need a job. Even one that is not a real job. Even one that is only volunteering.

81

STARVING MICE EATING PEOPLE

The cathedral has a unique desert highland theme. Its primary colors are a roguish purple and a hungry old gray. Its saints are made of sandstone and it's stained glass windows are scenes of relentless desert brutality: snakes eating mice, mice eating insects, insects eating corpses of snakes. Starving people. Starving children. Starving mice, snakes, and insects.

THE PARROT MAN

The cathedral is located on a hill that overlooks the city. On top of the hill is a graveyard and at the top of the graveyard is a manicured forest that belongs to the parrot man. Every morning on the top of the hill, on the top of the graveyard, in the middle of the forest, the parrot man trims his trees and cleans away brush and looks at the parrots he keeps there, to inspect for damage. If a parrot has been damaged in the night, the parrot man repairs it with bits of colored sand and blocks of soapstone he keeps on hand for the purpose.

The parrot man is private and his parrots are all in fair condition. The manicured forest is quiet and the trees are all in fair condition. The graveyard is somber and it's headstones are all in fair condition.

When we feel lonely, the mastiffs and I go up to the top of the hill, to the top of the graveyard, to the center of the manicured forest and we sit with the parrot man, for company.

THE STONE MASON

Now I live in the shape of a triangle and the third point of the triangle is a point in the middle of the university. When we all go together, I leave a trail of mastiffs, pecans, and the occasional blackbird behind me in a triangle shape that ends at the university, at a large brick commons with a fountain in the center. In the fountain there are catfish the size of mastiffs. The mastiffs look over the crenelated edges of the pool and they say, "Jah," in respect and fear. And the catfish look up at the mastiffs from the cool green water and they say, "Sho," in respect and fear. There hasn't been an incident yet, but the tension is palpable.

In the brick square, beside the fountain where the mastiffs say, "Jah," and the catfish say, "Sho," there is a stone mason who is always repairing the mosaics and replacing stiletto-pocked gold inlay. He pries out the buttery, craterous metal, and he pours in a new piece from the little gold smelting pot he keeps on his belt.

"One day we'll pilot an 18th century replica tall ship together and teach ancient mariner's star chart navigation to children in all sorts of places around the world," the stone mason tells me, as he is spreading the cooling gold from one brick to the next.

"One day we'll travel to the veld of the southern cape of Africa and release our wild bodies into the brush to make fire with sticks and make primitive sounds and strip down our flesh to only the bare and necessary parts and make savage love as just two sets of genitals, covered in sand and rust colored clay until the native people see us, and know us, and take us in. We'll drink the blood of cows we walk beside, mixed with their milk and slowly starve together, all together."

This is one of the stone mason's more gothic predictions. I say I am happy in the mastiff house.

He asks about the cathedral.

The cathedral is fine. There is a room full of bones where the priest makes lemonade. It's a queer practice. The bones are piled high. The lemonade is always refrigerator-cool. But I digress.

The fact of the matter is, the stone mason is in love with me and I have never been loved before, which is to say the stone mason has a feeling but I am too far away to feel the feeling, or to know about it at all.

CENTER WALKER

There is a concrete parking structure where the mastiffs go for fun. They run and stumble and climb up the one side, then slide on their backs and bellies all the way down to the exit.

They do this alone and in company.

Most times, it is just me and the mastiffs. Sometimes spectators come. Sometimes people using the parking garage for the usual purposes are taken aback by a sliding, gleeful mastiff saying, "Jah!"

One day, sitting alone on top of the concrete parking structure, amid howls and exclamations of "Jah," from the mastiffs, I meet a man selling candy corn from a big glass bell on a rolling yellow cart.

It is snowing.

The glass bell is frosted with snow flakes and the candy corn inside is glittering colorfully.

The man is called Piccolo and his arms and legs are long enough to wrap around his body twice, or even three times.

We talk about the weather and we eat the candy corn and we listen together to the mastiffs howl and yell with joy.

"Jah, weeee!" They yell.

"Jah, here I come!" They scream in delight.

Piccolo has eleven sisters and he says he makes the

candy corn with water from their tears. They cry around the clock since their mother died, and their tiny tears are sweet and cool and perfect for crafting candy. Piccolo does not cry.

The story of Piccolo is that he was born a sister. Or his mother, after eleven daughters, was not about to change the gender pronoun she used to refer to her children for just one child.

He wore handed-down dresses with embroidered cuffs and lace on the hems to make them longer as he grew. He wore denim jeans with sequins that the sisters sewed together. They all called him sister, he called them all sister. They bathed all together in a great plastic tub with handles shaped like begonias and creamy ocean waves painted on the sides.

"Piccolo, you will grow up to marry a sailor," said the sisters.

"Piccolo, your womb will be the most fertile and you will have eleven daughters," they said.

"Piccolo, your face will someday soften and your eyelashes will one day grow and your genitals will recede until you are just like us," they said.

"Piccolo, don't worry, you will be just like us. Because we all started out just like you," they said.

But those things, as lovely as they sounded, turned out not to be true. Piccolo knew no sailors and he met no sailors. His womb was no womb at all. His face never softened, but hardened, and on his twelfth birthday, a beard began to grow.

The beard was a source of judgment and concern.

His genitals enlarged and swelled with blood at random.

Peaches erupted from him unannounced and the beard grew and grew and grew.

The lithe pale bodies of his sisters transformed into meals that his genitals wanted to eat. The more they danced around, the hungrier he was. The more they called him sister, the more the beard reached out with all its might. The more the beard reached out, the more the peaches cascaded all down from him.

When they all ate together, they couldn't eat the peaches fast enough.

When they all walked together, they walked upon a carpet of peaches.

When they all bathed together in the plastic tub, it was a tub of peaches.

"Piccolo, don't worry, we all sprout some fruit sometimes too," they said.

But the sisters grew wary of the beard as it grew to cover them all in their bed at night. It was like a blanket of soft mold and they grew to calling it, euphemistically, Moses.

When their mother died, the sisters all received the Gift of Tears. And they cried until their crying was invisible and automatic.

Piccolo's peaches dwindled, but Moses grew and grew into a cavernous home.

Then one day, the eleven sisters knew it was time and they all clambered one by one into the soft folds and tangles of Moses. They helped each other nestle in against the pale forest cheeks of Piccolo, their sister.

Then Piccolo had eleven daughters all his own who were his sisters. His genitals swelled less often. The peaches that erupted from him grew more infrequent.

There was no mother, and Piccolo was alone with a weeping beard that he called Moses, and just a few scarce peaches.

But I digress. The fact of the matter is that Piccolo is in love with me and I have never been loved before. He is erupting peaches and I can see his sister-daughters parting his beard to say, "come on, there's a lot of room."

But I'm pretty happy in the mastiff house. So I decline.

MASTIFFS

It's possible that at first I did not notice the declining mastiff population in the house. If there was more room, or less drool, or less mastiff droppings, or more silence at night, or more pecans in the pecan trees, I could never say when the trend began. I could never say how long they have been leaving or going or being taken.

THE PARROT MAN

One evening in the manicured forest, the parrot man draws down a big wooden barrel from the canopy. It is suspended there with a system of complex and invisible pulleys, which he pulls and drops and balances as the barrel descends.

"Hey listen," he says.

I listen. The parrot man has never spoken. His silence is my companionship and when the mastiffs bark he has the same look as his plaster parrots, a look which plainly says: I am silent so that any damage anyone ever does can be repaired.

"Listen. This is where I keep all my secrets."

He opens up the barrel and there they are, all his secrets. Some in the shapes of conch shells and bananas, some heavy like bricks and some clearly ghosting through the physical barriers of the others and making them all seem connected, even if they aren't.

"Go ahead," he says.

So I go ahead. I take a secret.

It is a fish bone. It is transparent at one end and at one end it is white.

I look at the parrot man. "Okay," I say. He is smiling in his heart, which is to say, he is smiling secretly. There are no outward signs of a smile. And perhaps I only know what is truly going on in there, in his heart, because I am holding his secret. But that's all speculation.

It's right around the time of the secret that I do start noticing the dwindling mastiff numbers.

On a brick pathway in the park, littered with chestnuts and twigs and crawling with tiny ants, I take out the secret of the parrot man and I let the mastiffs sniff it.

"Jah," they say warily, "Jah, ma'am, that's for sure."

MOST SUBTLE MASTIFF

Now their personalities begin to emerge. With fewer mastiffs in the house, I can see them individually when they run around and play together. I name them according to their personalities: Most Subtle Mastiff, Excellently Kind Mastiff, Intelligent But Wary Mastiff, Mastiff With Persecution Complex, Actually Persecuted Mastiff, Courageous Mastiff, and Suspicious Mastiff.

I also start to have an excess of pecans.

The ecosystem was in perfect balance when I arrived. Now there are not enough mastiffs. The predator / prey balance is upset. In this model, the prey is the pecan.

Pecans pile up in the corners of the yard and underneath my hammock. Pecans crowd the house and explode from every cupboard. Pecans roll around treacherously beneath our feet and I finally declare: we have too many pecans.

I give them to neighbors and I bring them to the cathedral, but no one needs this many pecans. The pecan needs of a community can only be so great.

I visit the animal shelter with a rented van full of pecans but they tell me mastiffs don't eat pecans, and anyway they've had a sale on large breeds and they're fresh out of dogs larger than this (they show me a rabbit).

That's not a dog, I say.

Exactly, they say.

WHETHER OR NOT THE PRIEST IS MAKING LEMONADE FROM THE REMAINS OF PREVIOUS VOLUNTEERS

At the cathedral I spend most of my time polishing and sanitizing the pewter and sweeping the cobwebs from the benches where no one ever sits because no one ever visits. I wonder if church attendance has dropped world wide or if this is an isolated issue. I ask a lot of questions. The priest says, "don't ask questions."

Here is a list of questions I have asked, to which the priest has answered only: "don't ask questions."

1. Are there any other volunteers?
2. What is in that room?
3. What is in that other room?
4. Is there any more pewter polish?
5. What time is the service?
6. Is there a service at all?
7. Does anyone ever come to the service?
8. Is this even a cathedral?
9. What is your name?
10. What is my name?
11. How long have these tadpoles lived in the baptismal font?
12. Why do I keep sanitizing this pewter?

13. Where do all these bones come from?

14. Why do you make this lemonade in here?

15. What is in that room?

16. What is in that other room?

17. Is that a human femur?

18. Is that human femur important to the process of making this lemonade?

19. Why is this lemonade so great?

THE SIMILAR MAN

The only regular patron of the cathedral service is a man almost exactly my shape and size. He comes on Thursdays and listens to the mass from a pew in the back of the nave, under an ambry which contains a disemboweled snake. He is not bothered by the mastiffs, who are the only other recipients of communion. (The mastiffs like the wafers, and they have a weakness for the wine.) The man is polite and kind. His alms are generous, and he leaves promptly after the service.

On all days I watch him go until one day I decide to watch him stay.

I have nothing to lure him back into the shadows of the cathedral, so I offer lemonade.

We sit in the confessional, I on the priest side and he on the sinner's.

I lower the screen and pass his lemonade through the window. It has a boney tartness.

The man takes a sip. I can see he too tastes this boney tartness. His nostrils flare in this one way that is so familiar to me, because it is the one way my own nostrils flare.

I immediately recognize that this is the most perfect example I have had so far of a person the same size and shape as me. Our seated shadows are of equal height, our profiles are similar, our nose hairs are of roughly equal length.

I take a few sidelong looks at him.

He takes a few sidelong looks at me.

I see that it has just occurred to him that I am the most perfect example he has had so far of a person the same size and shape as him.

We have so many questions for one another that asking even one would unleash a torrential flood of inquiry. There is only one question that is appropriately asked from within a confessional booth and that is: can I be forgiven? But no one wants to be forgiven. We only want to be alike to one another. Which is not a sin. At least not yet.

So we sip our lemonade in silence.

After a few sips I raise the screen again between us and all I can see of him is the silhouette making sipping sounds from the other box. All he can see of me is the image of St. Peter that is painted on the other side of the screen. And the small collection of animal bones that the priest has placed on the ledge of the window. A fish bone, a cat skull, a partial ribcage like an open screaming mouth.

The only question I end up asking as we sip our lemonade in silence is a question to myself: "how many mastiffs were there at first?"

There's no clear answer. I wonder if it's written somewhere on the rental agreement. If there was a rental agreement. If there was a rental agreement, it was used long ago for some other important task like making a paper snowflake or cutting out butterfly shapes to amuse the mastiffs. If there was ever an answer, it's a snowflake or a butterfly. If there was ever an answer, it's gone. And the man certainly doesn't know. No, he certainly doesn't know a thing about the mastiffs.

ALLIGATOR PIE

At the mastiff house, a neighbor comes to call and she is selling alligator pie.

"Jah!" Shout the dwindling mastiffs, "Jah we'll take it all!"

"Please be reasonable," I say.

Alligator pie is a particular favorite of the mastiffs whose natural proclivity for carnivorous eating is by no means satisfied by a diet of pecans (and to be honest, the occasional blackbird).

The neighbor holds her wares high above her head as she wades through a current of tender drooling mastiff mouths.

The alligator pies are fresh. Their alligator steam curls up from their artful slitted pastry crusts, forming clouds of tender alligator scent across the ceiling of the mastiff house.

I fear a riot. I fear a rampage. The neighbor is unconcerned. But I purchase three steaming alligator pies and the neighbor is grateful.

She is sending the money to her son, she explains, traveling in the Australian outback. Studying ornithology. It's hot there, and dry, and her son is in constant peril. Her son, she explains, is a waterfall.

A 600 meter waterfall with a narrow crest and a swift and misty leap. They don't have a lot of sympathy there, she says, for waterfalls. But he has his research. And he is so dedicated to his research.

Her son is a handsome waterfall. This comes from his father's side. She shows me a photo. The photo is of a handsome waterfall with a narrow crest, a swift and misty leap.

"Oh my," I say.

"Jah," say the mastiffs, although they only really care about the alligator pie and who knows if they can even see in two dimensions.

The neighbor leaves and before the door has closed behind her, the charity alligator pies are set upon by a host of brindle jowls.

Oh what happiness, they all seem to me to be saying, but the only sound is the sound of munching and scuffling.

At night the window is open and I am nestled inside the mastiff hammock, rocking quietly to sleep. Outside, the similar man is looking in.

Oh what happiness, I seem to him to be saying, but the only real sound is the sound of heavy breath that proceeds a deep and uninterrupted sleep.

UNDERCROFT

If it were up to him, the priest would give a sermon every day. He would rise with the sun, bathe with the tadpoles in the baptismal font, throw his hand-embroidered robe on over his still wet and naked flesh, and begin proselytizing right away. Then in the evening time, when any attending parishioners had been enlightened and forgiven, blessed, and dismissed, he would crawl down into the rooms beneath the chancel and brew the sweet lemonade elixir in a room of human remains, to the immortal sounds of Joan Baez's *Rust and Bone* long into the night.

But the priest, like everyone, has a supervisor. And the supervisor is neither a woman nor a man. So there is just one sermon. One sermon which may or may not contain the name of an unfamiliar god.

When in the course of a sermon, the priest names a god, the god's name is Island of Shame or Lemon Aspirin Buckshot.

In this day and age, parishioners are as hard to come by as fossil evidence that documents the descent of man. So most times, the parishioners are myself, the similar man, and however many mastiffs.

The similar man, who is a mirror image of myself, is so perfect an image of me that we are indistinguishable to the priest. He is the similar man or I am the similar man. Or we both are the similar man. So the priest bestows one of us with the body, and one with the blood.

Neither of us are saved, but each of us is partially saved. The similar man drinks the blood and I eat the body and the priest says as we leave among the mastiffs: "in the name of Island of Shame."

THE STONE MASON

Beside the stone mason, a mastiff waits for pecans. The stone mason is busy. The mastiff is still. Its tail is straight. It has not drooled in five minutes.

The mastiff knows it is being good. It knows a pecan is forthcoming. It's only a matter of time until this mastiff is rewarded for its calm demeanor and attention to detail.

The stone mason takes no notice of the mastiff. Few people ever do when there is only one.

The stone mason's work is hard. Much damage has been done to the fountain in the center of the university commons. In the stone mason's line of work, this is classified as an emergency. Well-meaning trees have shot out roots from various places around the square. They have shot out roots up into the walls of the fountain. The water in the fountain will drain. The catfish there will air-drown. Their pleasant "Sho," sounds will fade into gasps, and then into silence.

All that could happen in a world where the stone mason was not present. It's lucky that the stone mason is present. For the catfish. And the mastiff, who expects a pecan any moment now.

But the moments come and go. Moment after moment. Tink after tink of the stone mason's hammer.

After a time, the patience of the mastiff is tested. Over the course of time, the mastiff grows doubtful that the stone mason intends to reward it. Over time the hunger pangs a mastiff feels begin to effect the mastiff's overall temperament.

The whole situation seems unfair. A calm, respectable mastiff waiting patiently for its reward. A dedicated stone mason working tirelessly in defense of the lives of some catfish. A calm, respectable mastiff. A dedicated stone mason. Some endangered catfish.

But who is a mastiff to judge what is right or wrong? Mastiffs have no moral absolutes. Their world view is limited. Mastiffs have been called primitive, simple, and unthinking. They have no representation in government. They don't understand social pressure or wealth disparity. That is because all mastiffs are equally wealthy. Mastiff wealth is measured in pecans.

The mastiff scans the skies for a blackbird, but none are near.

His patience is stretched thin.

His patience is not patience anymore.

In an instant, he is not himself. He lashes out. He bites the pale ankle of the stone mason. It is a quick, clean bite.

The mastiff can barely believe what it has done. "Jah," it cries in fear.

The mastiff jumps up and bolts across the square, leaving a bloodied stone mason, shocked and angry, resting against a half-chiseled replacement brick on the southeast side of the fountain.

Damn mastiffs.

Damn all the mastiffs, thinks the stone mason.

MASTIFF CONSCIENCE

Mastiffs suffer no great weight of conscience for their ill doings. They have terrible short term memories. The mastiff is hungry after running so far. It re-enters the mastiff house in a state of blissful ignorance.

THE STONE MASON

In the hospital the stone mason says: "One day we will buy a blue house in the city and have a child we name Charity and grow old together on the stoop beneath an ugly flowering tree.

"One day we will take out loans and attend college courses and become educated and elite. Our degrees will be framed and our debt absolved by our brilliance when we enter into our chosen fields.

"One day we will open a flower shop and grow our own roses and deliver garlands day and night for babies, deaths, sports victories, anniversaries and charity functions.

"One day we will break down into pieces and lay aside our rakes and ploughs and writhe in the uncut grass until a golden chariot sweeps down from heaven and gathers us together and bears us up. But the chariot driver will mistake our parts and recombine us as not ourselves but combinations of each other that are part me and part you and we will dwell in a workless heaven as one person who is two people each. And neither of us will sweat or toil or have to masturbate ourselves alone ever again."

ANIMALS IN CAGES

There is no reason to cage a mastiff but that it has bitten a stone mason. The bite is the reason. But if asked the mastiff might say: injustice, pecans, blackbirds, Jah, or any other sort of thing that is not the bite.

A cage for a mastiff is a cage for its mind.

A cage for a mind is the saddest cage of all.

An even sadder thing is a mastiff caged while other mastiffs are free.

I want to stand and weep for my one caged mastiff, whom I now call Thaddeus, but the similar man is waiting impatiently outside, peering through the open veranda windows of the mastiff house. He will not come in. The mastiffs fear him and look at him in ways that indicate they might administer a bite if a bite was needed, in ways that indicate they could all be Thaddeus, alone and confused in a cage.

I give Thaddeus one last look through the bars.

"Jah, ma'am surely we have come to the end of times," he says.

"Jah," I say softly which, contradictorily, means 'no.'

THE SIMILAR MAN

The similar man makes a tour of the burning buildings of the city.

The first burning building is a residence. Neighbors are gathered around in stunned and jealous silence. The sky is dark and the fire reflects like the center of a peach in each eye of the similar man, making his whole face which was once so much like mine, a massacre.

But I am not afraid. Not yet.

His fingers are curled with delight, mine are curled with confusion.

No one dies in burning buildings here, the city has advanced beyond death by incineration. In fact, the only way to die in the city is by caffeine overdose or suicide.

One mastiff can be seen escorting a small child from the crumbling wreckage. "Good job!" I shout to my mastiff that was once my mastiff but now who knows.

"Jah, all in the course of duty," the mastiff says. That is its standard line.

The once-inhabitants of the building on fire are huddled on the sidewalk. They are not displeased. Once in a while, a house must burn. It provides essential nutrients to the soil, which will feed and nurture the seeds of other houses later on.

As soon as the ashes cool, little bits of domestic life will begin again to sprout. Lusher, more vibrant than before: a new toaster, sheets with higher thread counts, gardening tools with no rust stains and elegant mid-century furniture.

The look of contentment is already around the ashy faces of the home dwellers. The neighbors are huffing at the thought of new toasters which will not be theirs. The mastiff is treating a small child for shock. I am wringing my hands like a nervous person. The similar man is peach-eye mad.

The second building is a hospital whose north wing has gone up in a blast. More mastiffs are gathered around, weaving in and around the crowd of people looking on. They check monitors and gauges and make notes on patient charts, greeting us politely when they pass.

No one asks, "are those your mastiffs," or "where do they all come from," because by now a mastiff is a common sight. And not all mastiffs belong to me.

Before the night is over, we watch a church, a grocery store, a bakery, all smoldering and crackling. The similar man grows hotter and grayer with every burning timber, every crashing roof beam, every sparking lawn, every ashy mailbox, until he is no longer the reflection of my face I knew, but a glimmering magnet which compels us to walk closer, to look at each other with the brassiest, most lustful peach centers in our eyes. My growing sense of dread is buried by the swift current of these interchanges.

In front of the bakery, we collapse together like two sides of a tent in heavy wind. Onlookers laugh and mastiffs say "Jah," which in this case means, "no."

BARN SWALLOWS INDICATE A SHARED HISTORY WE'RE STILL RECONSTRUCTING
or
THE SIMILAR MAN IS FULL TO BURSTING WITH PROMISES WE'LL NEVER KNOW IF HE CAN KEEP

In the sweaty whiteness of our post-coital moments, the similar man reveals a hidden chamber in the left side of his torso. Beneath the rib cage, which swings open on delicate ivory hinges, is a watercolor painting of the two of us, facing each other in another life as a pair of barn swallows.

To me, I seem overwhelmed. To the mastiffs, I seem panicked. To the similar man, I seem happy and he says: "ANYWHERE I EVER GO, I WANT TO GO WITH YOU. WHATEVER I DO TOMORROW, I WANT TO DO WITH YOU. WHEN I SEE OR HEAR OR TASTE A THING, I WANT TO SEE OR HEAR OR TASTE IT WITH YOU. THERE IS NO OTHER ONE. THERE IS NO OTHER ONE."

The watercolor picture of two barn swallows flutters faintly in my hands and I think of all the times I hoped for someone to show me such a thing but all this suddenly seems dangerous and false, from the barn swallows to the ivory hinges. I wonder if I have the whole thing right. I wonder if I ever had the whole thing right when as a child I stared up into the nettles and craters of my popcorn-texture ceiling and prayed without knowing what a prayer was for a thing to come and sweep me out into a husk so I could blow off easy in the wind.

But I digress. The fact is that the similar man loves me and I have never been loved by anyone before and I cannot know or feel a feeling which is so distant to my own experience.

"COME PLAY WITH ME FOREVER. COME LIVE WITH ME FOREVER. COME AND SEE THE THINGS I SEE AND DO THE THINGS I DO FOREVER."

I look around at the mastiffs in fire hats and the smoldering bakery smelling of burned jelly.

What I truly imagine is the similar man, an unquenchable fire, and the waterfall son of my neighbor, an unending 600 meter plunge from a rocky and sudden knickpoint with a swift and misty leap, batching steam together in the Australian outback forever.

And that is what really happens. Eventually. It is already beginning to happen. I know, and all the mastiffs know.

But I am no longer happy in the mastiff house, so I accept.

SHO

Declining mastiff numbers indicate a great imbalance in the mastiff house. The pecan trees are buried in the sprouted seeds they have been producing. The blackbirds emigrate to Spain. My nightly hammock is empty and uncomfortable and I doubt the whispers of mastiffs will ever lull me to sleep again.

In the house of the similar man, all the walls and floors are blank until I enter. As I enter they populate with images from the inside of my heart: nests of cold white flowers, shelves and shelves of books with flaking leather spines, the ocean in a storm, perfectly even fingernails, yellow woods with eyes shining out from crinkling bark, snow falling in long meadows, orange slices laid out in concentric circles, almost-invisible fishing line sinking by dips into the calm glassy surface of a morning lake, dustpans that leave no stripe of dust behind on crisp and clean linoleum, drying sponges and sunbeams in a kitchen.

At the mastiff house, Thaddeus moans day and night, growing no fatter on his constant pity-diet of alligator pie.

The sorrow sounds of this friendly, caged mastiff ache my heart, but I know he can never be released.

The few other mastiffs still lingering around the house rarely speak at all. When they do they are as likely to say, "Sho," as "Jah."

The few other mastiffs still lingering are lingering into catfish. One has even sprouted a set of wirey barbels ringed in a poisonous slime that Thaddeus calls "melon juice."

My dreams are fueled by the waking nightmare of an emptying house and my days are fueled by the blissful and swallowed company of the similar man. He knows my schedule and he follows me around as a herd of eager mastiffs once did.

I do not travel in a storm of mastiffs like the skipper on a mastiff boat at sea.

I do not distribute pecans from a blackbird at my waist. The blackbird at my waist is no blackbird anymore and the pecan trees have stopped fruiting altogether.

The similar man looks at me through peach fire eyes that are exactly the same size and shape as mine.

We share much.

There is much to share.

THE PARROT MAN

On a Sunday I find myself alone. My cool feet carry me up past the cathedral to the top of the hill, to the center of a graveyard there, to the center of a well-manicured forest where plaster parrots hang silently among trees.

That fair, fine repair work that the parrot man has wrought is evidenced all around. No mastiff follows me. I am alone of mastiffs. But so I am also alone of the similar man, whose feet on Sundays are bound to the inside-heart images his house projects. He sits glued down, perfecting all my deepest dreams to fill the blankness that was inside.

Alone and alone, we sit together, the parrot man and me, looking up through the hazy canopy and all around.

What would it be like to be a parrot man?

What would the average day consist of?

What would you see?

What would you eat?

The answers are so simple, they are a secret. A secret which I have pressed tightly to the upper section of my thigh. A secret I have always had.

UNDERCROFT

It is a great fear of mine to end up fleshless on the floor of a room in the cathedral, a priest making lemonade with one or more parts of me.

The priest is open about this possibility, but I cannot stop volunteering. It was in the contract, and the contract is framed now, lined up with other contracts of other people who have volunteered here. Other people whose bones are now, most likely, part of the process of making lemonade.

Will I be a bone on this cathedral room floor?

Will lemonade be made of me, too?

"No, certainly not," the priest has been heard to say, "I say, certainly not."

"Are the bones here bones of other volunteers?"

It is the only question I can ask to which he gives an answer.

And I take that, myself, as a sign.

THE SIMILAR MAN

At a bird concert in the wilds of the city we leap from tree to tree together like primal things. Listening everywhere to the different, mixing songs and laughing as the branches sway and snap beneath us. We are causing a ruckus, we are causing a riot. The similar man catches me falling through the leaves of a yellow wood tree, three nightjars and a buffalo weaver hot on my tail. The ruckus is a bird ruckus. The riot is a bird riot.

THE SIMILAR MAN, THE PARROT MAN, THE STONE MASON, ME

I can count on one hand the number of times I have been persuaded to give up a mastiff, and this is all before the mastiffs began to disappear, began to be subsumed.

1 (index finger). A charity auction
2 (middle finger). A soot-stained orphan lonely for a companion
3 (unnamed finger). The death of a horse that pulled a little carriage around the park for tourists and teenagers on corny dates
4 (little finger). For grocery money one month when things were very tight

I can count without any hands the number of times I told a similar man, or any one, what kind of images make up the lining of my heart because this number of times is zero. But when I walk into the house of the similar man, here I am among the quiet things I keep there.

The similar man is in the shower. I let myself in and sit on the kitchen counter while silence fills all the rooms. I am being followed by the similar man, or he is following me, or we are following each other. It's hard to say. When he emerges in a steam cloud from the shower, we follow each other down onto the kitchen floor and slide in the shadows of my heart cascading down from every wall. Am I being used as a vessel or a secret-keeper. Am I being used as a mirror or a light.

"ANYWHERE I EVER GO, I WANT TO GO WITH YOU. WHATEVER I DO TOMORROW, I WANT TO DO WITH YOU. WHEN I SEE OR HEAR OR TASTE A THING, I WANT TO SEE OR HEAR OR TASTE IT WITH YOU."

CATHEDRAL BONE

The mastiff house is empty when I return. Only Thaddeus remains caged and wasting near the hammock where I was once surrounded by comfortable bodies and will now always be alone.

At the bird concert I can say I have learned one thing: the similar man might catch me 99 times I fall, but every hundredth time he drops me. What I am saying is that I LOVE the similar man but he has never been LOVED before and he can neither know nor ever hope to understand a feeling he has never had.

On the hundredth fall, I enter the mastiff house. Poor Thaddeus, surrounded by silence and the quiet "Sho" of catfish in the sink, the basin, and the bathtub.

Thaddeus will neither eat nor sleep. I will neither eat nor sleep. So I crawl into his cage and lie beside him, much as I once lay myself down beside the similar man. We talk in whispers, much as I once talked to the similar man.

Cathedral bones. Cathedral bones.

I take out the secret of the parrot man and look it up and down. It's so stark and obvious, so clean.

All of my secrets, if I have even one, were mastiffs and now I have just one.

The similar man has loved before and will always love, but not me.

And Thaddeus.

In captivity he has grown small, about the size of a rabbit and I can hold him in my lap and feel his hot body everywhere at once. His soft velvet ears, his round, prickly jowls, his squarish head. His little brindle legs.

We sit up through the night, lulled into a calmness by the hissing of "Sho" all around us, which is another way of saying silence.

ABBOT CURRY AND
THE PARROT MAN

At the top of the hill, at the top of the graveyard, in the center of a well-manicured forest, there has been a terrible accident.

Here is a list of things that happened in the forest to make Abbot Curry and the parrot man into one bloody wet mess among the parrots:

1. The parrot man lay beside his parrot repairing tools, quietly combing small white secrets from his hair and beard.

2. A great explosion echoed across the manicured forest, reverberating against the brushless lawn, bouncing from one loose-leafed tree to the next.

3. The remnants of an enormous hot air balloon careened down from the darkening sky, it's colorful neon bag in a state of partial collapse, driving the pendulous basket around and around as it fell.

4. The parrot man thought of the apocalypse about to fruit.

Abbot Curry was once an architect of dreams. He was a preschool teacher. When all the children grew and no more children were ever born to replace them, he retired from that immortal and mystical position. He never built a child's dream world ever again. And Abbot Curry took up the work of his father, and his father's father: house painting.

Here is a list of things that happened on a hill outside of town to make the parrot man and Abbot Curry into one bloody wet mess among the parrots:

5a. A house painter named Abbot Curry loaded his house paint into a balloon basket for transport.

5b. The balloon basket swayed and bucked as the mighty vinyl balloon inflated, blocking out the setting-sun sky.

5c. A house had to be painted.

5d. The house in question was to be a creamy soft lilac, the color of Abbot Curry's eyes.

Here is a list of things that happened in the skies above the well-manicured forest to make two similar men into one bloody wet mess among the parrots:

6. The plummeting balloon basket glanced off high branches.

7. The dizzy occupant of the basket shouted. He was shouting the details of the last dream world he was ever tasked with building, the immaculate dream world of a small boy named Sam. The dream world architect is Abbot Curry. The listener is the parrot man. No one will end up alive.

8. "It is always night in the world but there are glowing mango trees instead of street lamps and no one ever dies. There are cars and giant dogs who graze on steak grass along the side of every narrow road. The birds are large and eat

the glowing mango lights until their tummies also glow and they fly around the sky, over the heads of the people who never die and the cars and the giant dogs."

9. The basket landed upside down in the arm of a tree.

10. The parrot man saw the architect of dreams clinging desperately to every paint can in the basket.

11. Their eyes pleaded with one another.

One said: "do not drop those paint cans."

The other: "I am going to drop these paint cans."

12. The paint cans dropped.

13. The tree-lodged basket was lodged in the tree of secrets. The half-deflated balloon collapsed.

14. The paint cans dropped.

15. The paint cans dropped.

16. The paint cans dropped.

17. There were no unscathed parrots. There were no untainted parrots. There were no unscathed dreams. There were no untainted dreams.

18. Abbot Curry was dead.

19. The parrot man was dead.

20. The last child's last dream world was dead.

And this is how I find the manicured forest: painted lilac when I wander into it at the top of the hill.

Should I even gather these defiled secrets or bury these lilac men I find covered in each other's bodies?

Lilac parrot eyes look on.

The hollow gold brown mastiff eyes I knew once too look on.

But they look peaceful, and I am happy in the heart-image house, so I leave.

THE STONE MASON

The stone mason has stepped his last foot off shore. Thank goodness all that is over.

He wishes someone would come to see him off, but there is no one and that is fine.

The stone mason is tasked, as his feet meet the planks of the tall ship, with giving himself a new name. He will never mend a stone again. And all the catfish are dead or changed to mastiffs (which is the same as saying dead).

So the stone mason calls himself, Her Hair. And Her Hair's feet are planted firmly on Her Hair's brilliant wooden tall ship. One foot is a foot and one foot is a carved wooden claw. He names the claw. He is in the mood for naming. He names the claw: Her Smile.

He names the tall ship Her Sex and the sea Her Grace and his crew he names Her Sad Eyes and he names the great pilot's wheel that he grasps with both hands Her Name.

Her Sex sets out on Her Grace, manned by Her Sad Eyes, and piloted by Her Hair, clutching Her Name.

What a lovely day, the last day.

We'll never see land again.

CENTER WALKER

In the snow-dusted glass bell of candy corn, a reflection of the similar man (or me), can be seen. Old peaches litter the cement, nothing but a lumpy brown paste watered by tears that leak from Moses.

And I miss the sounds of my mastiffs sliding down the one side of this parking structure, and clambering back up the other. "Jah, weeeeee, mistress," they would say, "Jah, ma'am."

UNDERCROFT

In the depths of the undercroft- far below the transept, in a small black room full of human remains, I am emptying shelves in search of pewter polish.

The priest is nowhere to be found. This is the hour he pretends to tune the pipe organ. This is the hour he typically lurks and spies. But today he is not around. Today he is absent.

I have left the pews fully dusted and cobweb-free upstairs in case he returns. A blackbird is standing solemnly in the murky green waters of the baptismal font waiting for me to give it a task, or for its brethren to return from Spain, or for the frogs to come back and make more tadpoles for it to eat.

Behind the first shelf is a tall stack of pickled beets. There is an eyeball swimming in one jar. There is an unmistakable toe in another.

Behind the second shelf are an array of dusty cans labeled "Preserves" but in a sinister way … like the ends of the letters are shaped into little bones and the capital P is a skull.

Behind the third shelf is a thing I never thought I'd see. It is the similar man.

His face is the exact size and shape of my face.

His hands are curled up with gleefulness.

His eyes are peach fires. Or I am imagining they are

peach fires, though they are as black and hollow and empty as the drained fountain in the college square where catfish once 'Sho'd and the stone mason once worked.

But I know him, finally, by the delicate door on little ivory hinges that opens into where a heart would be, if there were any organs at all. Which there are not and have never been.

I am stumbling back from the thing I don't want to see.

I am tumbling over bones away from the bones I can't keep seeing.

I am taking a stack of "Preserves" with me on my way down into the bones.

The priest, at the door, clears his throat.

WHEN ALONE, THE SIMILAR MAN
AND HIS HOUSE

The similar man's house is deserted.

The backs of my hands are still flaky with lilac paint from the forest. When I turn the handles of every door of every room, small chips of lilac fall like flower petals marking a path I have romantically traveled, all along the interior of a blank-walled space that was once bursting with colorful images of the inside of my heart.

In one room of the house there is a blackbird. The blackbird is exactly the same size and shape as me. It's wings are frosted white and red at the tips with the remnants of sand that it flipped through, and the remnants of ice that it touched. It's boot lacquer beak is loaded with pecans as gifts for mastiffs I no longer have.

The fact of the matter is that, the way the blackbird loves me is not the way that something loves another thing really. It wants all of my mastiffs gone. It wants all of my company lilac. It wants me to dance and jump around and spread wide open and fall 99 times but it doesn't want me to fall the hundredth. I know because this blackbird in the house of the similar man, is the similar man.

Thaddeus is so small now I have transferred him to my pocket. I can feel him whispering there and breathing. I know if he could, he would already have run away. But we both have a deep respect for the law. And Thaddeus must be caged. Whether behind bars or in a pocket, it makes no difference.

The breaths of Thaddeus become as nuanced and clear as a high quality vinyl pressing of a mastiff breathing.

I am staring at the blackbird / perfect man. The blackbird / perfect man is staring at me.

I know, even though I could never know.

I know this house is meant for someone else. Even when the blank walls filled up with perfect images that I recognized and loved, the whole thing was meant for someone else. My lilac petals are already melting in the heat and they are the only stain I'll ever leave behind here.

When I am lemonade and one of many bones, I will think about the two barn swallows. I will think long and hard. And eventually, I'll find that that second barn swallow was never me, neither was the first. The organs designed for feeling hurt by this knowledge will already be gone, so I won't even cry or think of crying. But Thaddeus will.

WE ALL SET THE
HOUSE ON FIRE

Mastiffs pile down from the fire engines before they reach the burning house. They switch on their hoses and break out their axes and rush around shouting commands and sniffing in the grass.

But they all know it's too late.

This burning house is an endless fire, fueled by a self-combusting blackbird.

They call the only person they know who can help.

WATERFALL

A never ending waterfall, a student of ornithology studying abroad in the Australian outback, receives a call.

The call is from his mother.

His mother is distressed.

He can hear the sound of people saying "Jah" everywhere around her through the telephone receiver. He can hear the sounds of slurping and gulping associated with eating an alligator pie.

Then, far in the distance of these sounds and other sounds and his mother's voice, is the sound of fire crackling and he understands. It's time to go home at last.

ABOUT THE AUTHOR

Kirsten Alene is the author of *Rules of Appropriate Conduct* (Civil Coping Mechanisms, 2015) as well as three other books published by Eraserhead Press. She lives on the Oregon coast in a small blue house with her husband and daughter.